WARNING

This book contains sexually explicit scenes and adult language. It may be considered offensive to some readers. This book is for sale to adults ONLY.

Please store your files wisely where they cannot be accessed by underage readers.

* * * * * * * * * * * * * * * * * * * *

WANT FREE COPIES OF MY BOOKS?

Just visit my blog and download free copies of my books:

http://gideon-elliot.awesomeauthors.org/gideon-elliot/

About the Publisher

4Fun Publishing, a member of **BLVNP Incorporated**, 340 S. Lemon #6200, Walnut CA 91789, info@blvnp.com / legal@blvnp.com

NOTE: Due to the highly emotional reaction of some people to works of erotic fiction, any email sent to the above address that contains foul language or religious references is automatically deleted by our anti-spam software and will not be seen. All other communications are welcome.

DISCLAIMER

Please don't be stupid and kill yourself. This book is a work of FICTION. Do not try any new sexual practice that you find in this book. It is fiction and not to be confused with reality. Neither the author nor the publisher or its associates assume any responsibility for any loss, injury, death or legal consequences resulting from acting on the contents in this book. Every character in this book is over 18 years of age. The author's opinions are not to be construed as the opinions of the publisher. The material in this book is for entertainment purposes ONLY. Enjoy.

Blue Identity

Gay Erotic Romance

GIDEON ELLIOT

Blue Identity

5-Book Box Set
Gay Erotic Romance

By: Gideon Elliot

© Gideon Elliot 2015
ISBN: 978-1-62761-357-6

Blue Identity

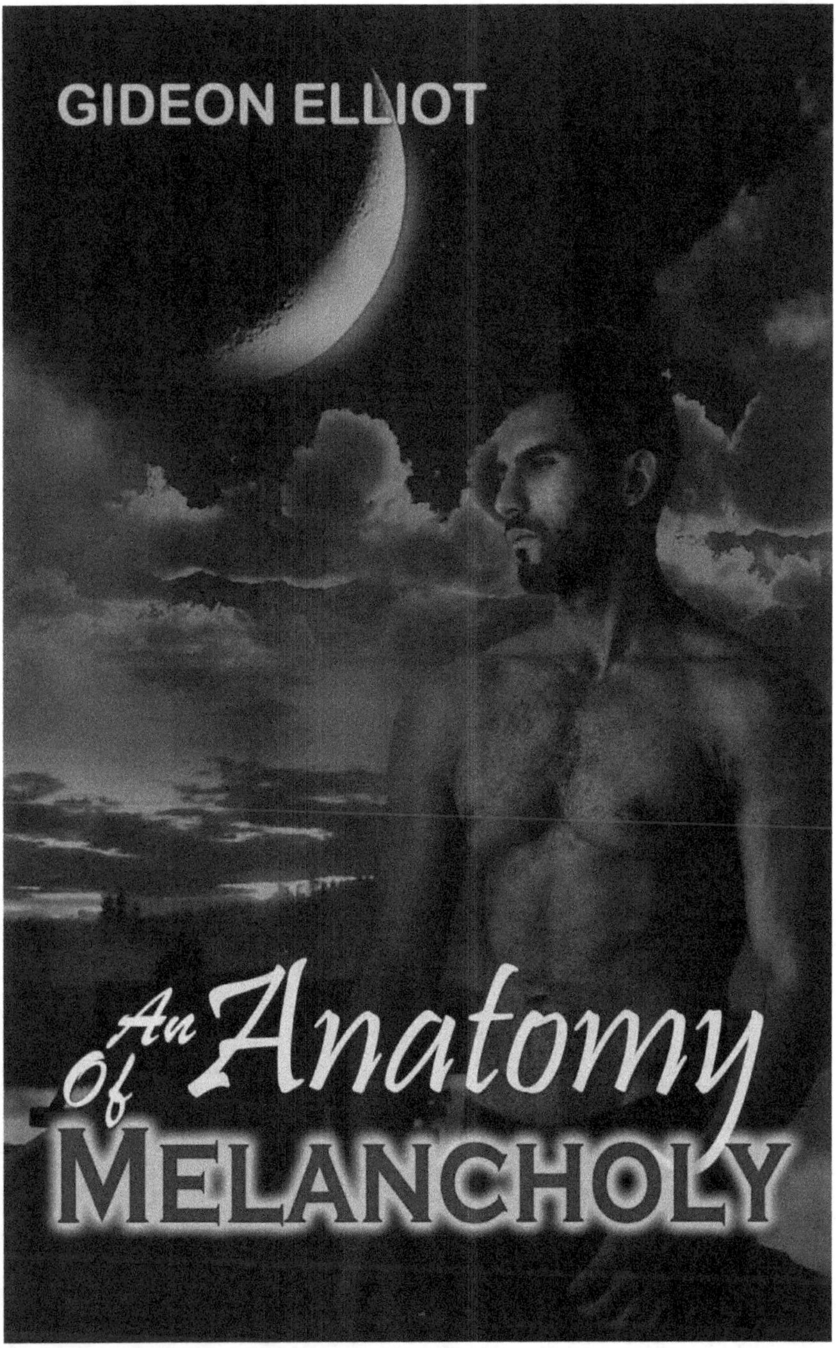
GIDEON ELLIOT
An Anatomy Of
MELANCHOLY

An Anatomy of Melancholy

There was nothing more I could do. He was gone and I knew there was no way I could bring him back. Perhaps that was a good thing. Perhaps it wasn't.

What I could do was take a shower, scrub myself down, shave, get dressed, go out and get a haircut, buy some new clothes, work out at the gym, go for a drink at Benny's, stop in at the new sushi place on Barrow Street, get home around midnight, get stoned, listen to Jauchtzet Gott in Allen Landen, the Schwarzkopf recording, jerk off, and get some sleep. Tomorrow morning I'd go into work.

It would keep me busy. It would keep me going. And that's really all that mattered after all.

***

ELLEN WAS waiting for me on the doorstep when I got home.

"You look better than I expected," she said.

"What did you expect?"

"A wreck," she said.

"Sorry to disappoint you," I said.

"I'm not disappointed," she said. "I'm glad. Anybody after almost ten years..."

"What are you doing?" I said, quietly.

"What do you mean?"

"You know perfectly well what I mean."

It never failed. She was getting me angry. The last thing I needed. It was a trick of hers. But I caught myself in time.

"I don't want to do this, Ellen," I said with no affect.

"You don't want to do what?" she said.

She was baiting the hook. She'd use any response as a way into a fight. Fighting was foreplay for her. I wasn't having it, and I wasn't going to explain. Even that was a way of involving me. I wasn't even going to explain why I wasn't going to explain.

"Good night, Ellen," I said unlocking the door to the building.

"You don't know what's good for you," she said, on the verge of crying.

It wasn't going to work.

"Perhaps," I said. "But I'll deal with it. Good night." I let myself in and disappeared behind the door, closing it gently behind me, leaving her there.

Actually, I felt better than I thought I would.

**

UPSTAIRS, I lit a joint, turned on the cd player and the blatting baroque trumpets of 51 began shouting. I took the underwear I'd bought out of all the wasteful cardboard and plastic packaging. Three pairs, all black: hip hugging, low rise boxer briefs, bikini briefs, and a thong. A cock ring, too. I stripped, snapped on the cock ring and put on the thong. The feel of the elastic string in the crack of my ass made me stand straight. I held my balls -- tight in the silky microfiber -- in the palm of my hand and let out a great sigh.

I looked in the mirror. Abs, glutes, pecs, eyes, hair, nipples, basket, thighs, everything. I would have gone home with me in a flat second if I'd passed me on the street.

I walked to the window. There was a curtain covering only the bottom half, so nobody across the street could see below my chest, but I could always see the sky.

There was Tony standing by the window across the street. When he saw me he grinned and picked up his cell and mine rang.

"Yeah," I said, "come on over."

***

HE DIDN'T bat an eye, just took hold of my shoulders, drew me to him and kissed me gently on the lips.

I handed him the joint and he took a toke, deep in and let out a long stream of smoke.

"Is it ok if I ask how you're doing?"

"I don't mind if you ask," I responded, "but it drives me crazy from just about anybody else."

I snuggled my head in the hollow formed where his neck met his shoulder and he gently rocked me in his arms.

"How are you doing?" he whispered.

"I'm ok," I said. "There really isn't anything I want to talk about. What people can't seem to understand is that talking creates a kind of fiction. And you get attached to that. I'm quiet. Things move. So do I."

He held me at arm's length and smiled.

"You want to see the suit I got?" I finally said, grinning.

"I'm not sure," he said. "You look great in next to nothing."

It was a great suit and I knew I looked terrific in it, but the best was when Tony slowly undressed me afterwards, looking deep into my eyes, undoing my tie, a rich burgundy, unclasping the diamond collar pin, taking out the matching diamond cufflinks, unbuttoning the pale saffron shirt, slipping off the three button jacket, dark blue with a faint burgundy pinstripe, undoing the narrow belt, removing those ultra-supple black calf skin Perlini shoes that were lighter on my feet than gloves and my high black socks with the nearly invisible diamonds woven into them, then my trousers, until I was back to only a thong.

Then his tongue played over my nipples and my cock strained against the thong until he lowered it. His hand delicately closed around my scrotum, tight with the texture of a walnut shell. He kneeled in front of me and licked my balls and took them into his mouth and caressed them with circling tongue strokes.

As he sucked my cock he kneaded the muscles of my ass but kept me on the brink so that he could give himself to me on his back. I mounted him and slowly fucked him. We kissed slowly and interrupted our kisses to gaze at each other as I kept going into him and he kept receiving me until I became incandescent. Lashes of his semen whipped my chest and our breath was a storm which raged like a hurricane along the plains of our valleys and upon the ranges of our mountains. The thunder roared and darts of lighting tore through us. We had become nothing but sky.

The tempest was wild in our breaths as we kissed until the raging winds subsided.

"Remember," Tony said, as we lay together calmly afterwards sharing a joint the way years before lovers used to share a cigarette; "anything you need. I'll always be here for you, no matter what. Even if you just need the soles of your feet licked."

"I know," I said, stubbing out the joint, and kissed him before we fell asleep.

***

WHAT THE hell am I supposed to do with this?" Gunther moaned between clenched teeth.

"You're supposed to print it in next week's issue," I said.

"I can't do that," he said with an attempt at innocent exasperation.

"Why not?" I parried.

"Because it's a blatant piece of corporate disinformation. I don't care how prestigious the byline."

"O, Dexter," I said laughing, "when will you get over being skittish?"

"Now, what's that supposed to mean?" he shot back momentarily forgetting the matter at hand.

"You've got to remember," I said, ignoring the tangent we had bumped into and ploughing ahead, that the magazine has been bought. "You don't publish it anymore. You have no say about its content. Think of yourself as more or less an administrative editor. Absorb yourself in problems of grammar and punctuation, sentence structure and syntax."

"And since when have you become so cynical, Matt?"

"I'm not cynical. I'm just aware of what the world actually is like."

"That's what I mean. That's cynical. You know that better than anyone. The world isn't like anything. The world is what we make it or what we let it become when we give in and give up."

"What do you want me to do?"

"How about we both walk out on this job?"

"You mean quit the magazine?"

"Not if we don't have to, but, yes, if it comes to that. Give them a fight first."

***

SO THERE we were in the oak paneled board room.

Both Henry Pinchons were present, Senior and Junior. Senior was a blustering bully who demanded absolute obedience. Corpulent and bilious, he was a grand sensualist with a voracious appetite for power and a lust which sated itself on commanding and dominating. He owned a movie studio, a radio network, sixteen newspapers, a dozen television outlets, an internet content provider, and fourteen magazines. It was rumored he was in negotiations to buy one of the baby Bells, and he was building cell phone towers in Iraq.

Junior was his lieutenant, the moon to his sun, his youthful mirror and a reminder that Senior, as repulsive physically as he had become by the way his monstrous appetite had deformed him, that Senior had once been an eyeful. Junior's good looks and gym-built body were undercut by the want of an independent spirit. You could see in Junior, nevertheless, where the self-assurance, which Old Pinchon had drained from his son, had come from. In the old man it had been amplified by the strength of his will. In Junior, that same will had been the force that undermined him.

Myra Daley was present, too, very elegant in a cobalt blue Armani skirt suit with a double breasted jacket over a bare bodice, set off by a string of pearls. She looked at everything; she looked through and beyond everything with steel gray eyes. She had tight, thin lips, red hair, and she never spoke. She just watched and made notes. She had long fingers adorned with several gold rings and a brilliant ruby, and she had almond shaped nails which were painted a bright Chinese red. She was Pinchon's lawyer, and most people thought she was his mistress, too, but I guessed she played a shrewder game than that.

Two guys in dark mustard green suits, real bruisers, whom I'd never met before were also present. They were introduced by name. One was from the State Department; the other, from the Attorney General's office. Their handshakes hurt.

I realized -- metaphorically speaking -- that they had drawn their guns, and I was curious to see in which direction they were aiming to shoot. My guess was ours.

The author of the piece was not present.

"As a publisher," Pinchon said, looking at Dexter with affable contempt, "I'm not in the habit of insulting my writers." He drew slowly on his Garcia-Vega and then added, "certainly not one of the stature of Brian Arthur."

"And as a writer," Gunther shot back, "I learned long before I became an editor that I could not take a challenge to my writing as an insult to my person. I thought that the foundation of democracy was argument whether it's with the guy next door or the president's chief of staff."

"But you want to prevent that argument from taking place in the pages of my magazine," Pinchon said with triumphant composure.

"No, sir," Gunther rejoined. "There is no argument when the possibility of rebuttal is denied, as it is in the pages of -- your magazine."

"We are the rebuttal," Junior piped in with a line of right wing agit-prop he had picked up.

His father scowled at him.

But I winked at him. He was cute, and I thought he'd be a much better bedmate than a political philosopher. He blushed as if he knew what I was thinking. Perhaps he did. There might, in that case, still be hope. I don't mean only for seducing him. I mean for social change. Maybe. But, then again, maybe not. Not while his father was still alive. And then, too, you could never know how deep the old man was embedded in him. Probably he wasn't just closeted; more likely he was coffined.

***

"**WE DIDN'T** budge and they didn't budge. So we fired each other. Except they got to keep the magazine and all its assets. We got to keep the sort of integrity you get by giving up high paying corporate jobs, which in the eyes of most people makes you seem like an ass."

Dexter Gunther was manic again, as that last utterance -- which he unloaded around a table of our friends at Crazy Benny's late Friday night while Nick the pianist segued from "Love for Sale" to "It had to Be You" -- demonstrated.

Then Tony came by and asked me to dance when Nick started to play "Easy to Remember." The giant mirrored ball turning on the ceiling made glints of silver shimmer in circles around the room. He held me close and, I know it's corny, but we got lost inside each other. Then Nick went into "Every Time We Say Good-bye." We kissed as we danced. It was that kind of night. We got quite tipsy on cognac at the bar. Tony met a leather guy who couldn't keep his eyes off him and went home with him.

Dexter was still manic, but that was habitual with him. This time he was incubating a new magazine. I could tell something was up even before he told me. His brain never slept and he always came out on top. He left with a green-eyed, brown-haired skinny kid who was all muscles and bones and had the sweetest smile you'd ever see, and skin finer than silk.

I walked around for a while afterwards and drifted down to the Morton Street pier at the edge of the Hudson. It was deserted. I smoked a joint and watched the crescent moon shine high in the sky above the river. I felt an all-encompassing sense of emptiness, of nothing, of sheer vacancy embrace me.

End of the 1st book

The Dialectics of Slavery:
The Ideas and the Realities

THE END OF NOTHING

GIDEON ELLIOT

The End of Nothing

"It's the end of nothing," Avram Chernovsky said, sitting at the oil-cloth covered kitchen table in the old, ill-lit kitchen in a Moscow suburb as he bit into a piece of tea-soaked sugar and lifted the hot glass of strong tea to his lips.

"Nothing! Heed what I say." Chernovsky looked at Miriam, his wife, although, in fact he was addressing his only son, Elijah -- but in school, he was called Sergey -- aged ten, attempting to moderate the boy's excitement, which, it seemed, the entire population of Russia shared since the fall of the wall in Berlin, city of un-numberable deaths.

"Nothing! It's always the same. We go from constriction to chaos and back to constriction again. And chaos, chaos they think is freedom. Freedom!"

He attacked the word, yelling it in a whisper, and was quiet.

"Well," he said after a moment, reflectively, "maybe some good can come out of it."

***

HE KISSED the ground, the hard concrete, of the American earth after they passed through customs at Kennedy and emerged into the gloomy daylight of a rainy September.

"Papa," Elijah, said.

"And why shouldn't I?" his father said, standing. "This is not nothing."

They found the bus to the Port of New York Authority Bus Terminal on Eighth Avenue and Forty-second Street, and that was all their sojourn in New York City. The bus there took them up to the depot on Main Street in Burlington, Vermont, in front of the bagel bakery, where they were met by a young woman in a Russian peasant blouse and a wind-breaker from the Vermont Refugee Resettlement Association. It was balmy and the middle of September and the blazing leaves were still on the trees, and the color of everything kindled a blaze in Avram's soul.

They found an apartment in the Old North End, bigger for sure than in Moscow, and Elijah -- now in school also called Elijah -- had his own room with a backyard window looking onto a small forest with an elm tree stark in its bareness from the blight which had killed all the elms.

Miriam worked at the City Hall as a computer programmer and Avram delivered bread for an artisan baker located in Craftsbury, driving up I 89 to Craftsbury at four each morning in an old Subaru station wagon that had only squeaked through inspection, and stopping on the way back in St. Johnsbury, Montpelier, Richmond, Williston, South Burlington, and Burlington to make deliveries.

At night, he practiced his English by reading *War and Peace* in translation, sometimes to himself, but sometimes out loud when Miriam or Elijah or both of them would sit with him around the kitchen table, a large pine table in a large, well-lighted kitchen, which had a plank wood floor and a door going out to the back steps, which went down to the garden, where Avram grew tomatoes and zucchini in the summer and Miriam planted daffodils and tulips and roses and irises.

***

ELIJAH GREW into a well-knit, young man, tall and handsome, thick sandy hair, blue eyes, intellectual, athletic, and friendly with everyone. He played the violin in the Vermont Youth Orchestra and was captain of the swimming team at school. There was hardly a cool head in the house or a heart that did not leap at the end, when he was the soloist for the First Violin Concerto by Shostakovich at the Flynn Theater; and when he stood at the edge of the Olympic sized pool at the swim meets at Burlington High School in his tiny speedo, there was no eye that could take itself off him.

At night he dreamed of his team mates but their young and wonderful bodies were bound in chains and straps of buckled leather. Sometimes, he ran frightened through the woods or swam under the earth in a stream that became a secret tunnel, and real music, French horns playing Mozart, filled the ears of his mind. Sometimes it was terror, and sometimes the white fluid of night shot through his loins and made him fly with angel wings.

"Avadim ha-yinu l'pharo b'mitz-raim."

"We were slaves unto Pharaoh in Egypt and to Stalin and Khrushchev and Brezhnev and Kosygin in Russia," Avram added as he chanted at the Passover seder.

"Slaves, always we have been slaves, but now, here, in America, we are not slaves. Even if we are workers, hard workers, we are not slaves. Especially then! We are free men. We shape our own destiny, and you, you," he said proudly grabbing Elijah's forearm and shaking it, "you are destiny I am shaping in new world, in America. Harvard, he's going to, my son. Ah, America!"

The word was a fetish for him. He could not say it enough. He caressed it in his mouth like a beloved object. America.

Elijah reached over with his other hand and covered his father's hand which still gripped his forearm and smiled. Avram's face relaxed into radiance and he looked around him at all his new friends at this communal table in this America of his and said, softly, even with awe, "My son!"

Afterwards, Elijah walked out with his parents and his school friend Benjamin. Avram and Miriam were going to walk home, but Elijah said that he and Benjamin would walk around for a while, perhaps down to the lake, for the late April night was warm and the moon was pale and bright and full in the sky.

Avram embraced him and kissed his cheek.

"It is already next year and we are already in Jerusalem," he said with a gleam in his eyes and a chuckle.

***

THROUGH THE trees along the hillside called Depot Street as they descended to the lake side, the young men saw the moon in the sky over the lake, and then once alongside the lake; they saw it twice, as the hypnotic disk in the heavens and as an undulous stripe reflected in the glassy sheen of the lake.

The path along the lake was deserted and the boards under their feet were sonorous with their footsteps, and they took hold of each other's hands.

They stopped at the railing and looked out at the lake.

Benjamin turned towards Elijah and, still holding his hand, placed his other hand behind his neck and drew him forward until their lips met in a long and delicate kiss.

Elijah felt cherished and desired and he gave himself with a gesture that felt like surrender to him, opening his mouth and yielding.

It was that sense of surrender, of yielding himself to his beloved Benjamin, the strong and perfect Benjamin, the only one of all his friends he thought his equal and in some things his superior, it was that sense of surrender that made everything they did maddeningly exciting.

"It is strange," he said, as they looked out to the New York shore in the far distance, "my father speaks so fiercely against slavery, yet when I am alone with you, all I wish for, all I feel happening within me is surrender, as if I wished to be enslaved to you. Command me and I obey," he teased, mocking himself.

"Kiss me," Benjamin ordered, and Elijah pressed again his lips to his and they shared their breath, which was their spirit, and Benjamin gently rubbed his palm across his boyfriend's chest and lingered there caressing his nipples.

***

IN SECRET, in stolen moments, in hidden or deserted places, they went together to the intangible secret and hidden places that exist within us in the dimensionless space of the mind, in the metaphysical crevices of memory, in the recesses of forgotten recollection.

On a late autumn day when the sky was heavy with storm clouds and lightning rent the cloth of the sky with jagged lines of incandescent barbed wire and the thunder rumbled in great reverberations, Benjamin sat on an old wooden chair in the brick and board attic of his parents' large house beside an old leather couch no longer in use but too good to throw away upon which Elijah was stretched out. Only a burning candle in an old bronze candle stick gave them light.

"You are becoming more and more relaxed. You are drifting, drifting into a deep hypnotic trance, drifting slowly, floating, sinking down, sinking into a great pool of memory, into a deep, deep trance and going deeper and deeper, deeper into a great pool of memory, you are floating in a lake of memories; all you hear is my voice. My voice is your guide -- my voice is your memory.

"Can you hear me, Elijah?"

"Yes."

"You are going deeper. You are going deeper into the pool of memories, and farther, farther back until you see yourself in childhood.

"Go back now, further back. You are a child in Moscow. What do you see? Tell me. What do you see? Tell me what you are seeing, Elijah."

It was early morning and they were going through the chilly streets where the women in babushkas were cleaning the pavement with straw brooms, and they turned into a dirty alley and went through a doorway without a door into an old tenement that looked like it must have been standing even when Dostoevsky was writing, and took their way up winding wooden steps to a small room with chipped plaster and a hissing radiator and one window with oil cloth where one of its panes should have been. The room smelled of boiled fish and boiled potatoes and boiled cabbage. A group of men was gathered there.

"I don't know," his father said, looking strained as he took a blue velvet bag with gold embroidery lions facing each other, rampant, stitched upon it from out a burlap sack full of buckwheat.

"What you don't know? He should know. It's time he should know. He should grow up without knowing? How would that be?"

"There will be worse things than that."

"I won't argue with you whatever you say as long as still and all you did bring him, and he will see and he will know."

What Elijah saw was the men with their arms bared, their shirtsleeves rolled up high almost to the shoulders; on the pasty white flesh turned in circles the shiny black straps of the phylacteries. It fascinated him with revulsion, except for one young laborer among them whose arm was not pasty like a rising dough but strong and brown from the sun and muscled with labor so that his muscles rippled like stones beneath the skin and the straps wound in a hypnotic spiral up his arm to his bicep and something stirred like desire within Elijah.

He saw, and a current vibrated within him, and he knew, but he did not yet know what it was he knew.

***

THEY PARTED in August, when Benjamin went to Stanford in California and Elijah went to Harvard in Massachusetts. Massachusetts! a word which gave Avram almost as much pleasure to say as America.

Time passed as it will whether one is a free man or a slave. Which is not to deny there is a difference! But what that difference was became the central concern guiding Elijah's thought. Indeed, it shaped his life. And what actually did that word, slave, mean? What did it point to? One thing, when his father used it; quite another, when it shook him to the roots.

He read Hegel and Bergson, majored in psychology and philosophy and took courses in management and labor relations. He went through the tedious tomes of Stalin and Hitler and Mao. He read the Marquis de Sade and the pornographic books of Guillaume Apollinaire. He read *Venus in Furs* by Sacher-Masoch. He studied hypnosis and went to a practitioner to learn it.

Instead of to the synagogue on Friday nights he went to The Leather House. Instead of phylacteries, he dressed himself in a polished leather harness. Instead of the reveries which are for some induced by tasting the ancient words carefully inscribed on the sacred scrolls he experienced the enchantment of the trances that the swooning words, obedience, submission, domination, and master work upon the sinews.

He knelt before a man who swung a chain before his eyes, and his mind was filled with the man's words and his acts became the ones the man suggested. He bowed and licked his boots and stood beside his bed and swooned as the man turned his nipples and said you belong to me and eye to eye penetrated him and filled him till he came.

***

"**WHAT!**" **HIS** father cried with a fearful shudder that rippled through him and stopped in his heart, when he saw Elijah the Thanksgiving of his junior year at Harvard when he came home for the weekend.

"What!" Avram cried when he saw the silver earring in the piercing in Elijah's ear.

"It is forbidden among us to do such things. It is the mark of a slave."

Elijah took his father in his arms and kissed his cheek and held him tight.

"No, Papa, no," he said. "Not in America. In America it is a mark of freedom."

"Of freedom?" incredulous the old man cried.

"Of freedom, Papa, of freedom from the fears, the superstitions, the customs, and the oppressions of an old world, of a different world, of a world we no longer are in. This is another time, Papa. This is another world."

Avram was torn. From his heart he wanted to cry, "All time is the same time. There is only one world and it is always the same."

And yet, it was he, was it not? who took his family to this America and behaved himself as if it were a different time, a new time in a new world. Had he not said it was already next year, and it was already Jerusalem? Was this what next year, what next time, looks like? he wondered, gazing at his son. Why not? Perhaps.

So he looked up at the strong and handsome, manly son who held him in his arms and said, "Perhaps it is as you say."

Elijah held him longer, kissed him again, then let him go.

"So Papa, a little vodka, no?"

"With ice."

"With ice."

"To the new time!"

***

AVRAM DANCED with joy when Elijah got his degree from Harvard and a teaching fellowship in New York City at Columbia, where he was going for his doctorate.

"His doctorate," Avram repeated, and the word was candy in his mouth.

And when, three years later, it was published -- *The Dialectics of Slavery: Between the Ideas and the Realities* -- Avram read it, although it made him dizzy, and, like Petrarch, his real pleasure came from caressing the book and gazing at the pages, turning them slowly one at a time, in awe, letting his eyes linger on each page seeing how the black print caressed the white paper.

End of the 2nd book

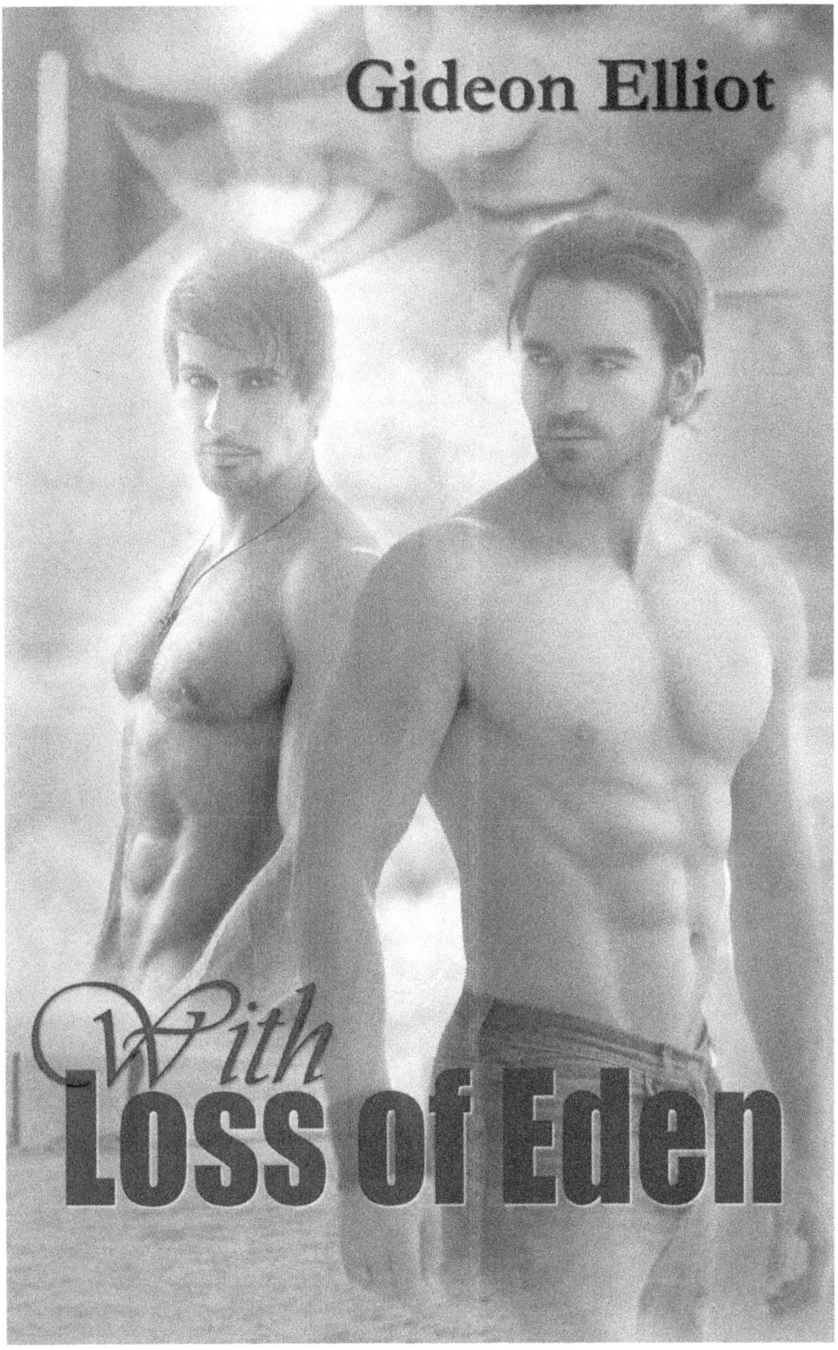
Gideon Elliot
With
Loss of Eden

With Loss of Eden

I was thinking the other evening of Brian Arthur -- Brian Arthur as he once was -- no less real than he is now, but before he became a nationally-known figure, famous as one of the chief architects of the current administration's military empire, and how we used to make love -- really -- inside the trucks which were parked under the old West Side Highway by the warehouses overlooking the shore of the Hudson River.

He always had a joint ready and a conspiratorial smile. I can picture him now, the way he looked that summer, hotter than most. Brian, of course, was always the hottest, but I mean the summer in that last sentence. Because of the heat his chest was always bare, shirt tucked away into the back pocket of his really short cut-off jeans, and because he loved to scamper along the rocks or jump from one of the gravel barges that lined the shore to another, the only other items of apparel he sported were a pair of high workboots, well-laced and a pair of thick gray socks. We were the same age, twenty-four. It was 1972. We were among the few who were voting for McGovern.

I met him in the gym at Sheridan Square over the West Side Savings Bank and next door to the Greenwich Village Peace Center, where we also hung out. He worked out for tone, not bulk, and was beautifully lithe, nearly hairless of body, and his eyes danced with light and laughter. He always seemed to be having a silent, internal conversation with himself which made him break out in mysterious smiles; it was impossible for him to keep himself from bubbling over.

"Hey," he said to me, one morning as we were changing back into street clothes.

"Hey yourself," I said with a grin, dumbfounded and shy, wanting to solder the contact but shy and inexperienced at this sort of thing, which was exactly what I was hoping would happen, but when it did, not knowing quite how to negotiate the rapids. Even in my fantasies, I always skipped from seeing my desired object to being on my knees in front of him with his cock in my mouth and my arms round his thighs.

But now I didn't have to say anything. I already sensed it. I was in the hands of a master. Charm was natural to him, and he had a knack for putting people at ease, for bringing them out.

"Hey, if you're free, walk down to the pier with me. It's going to be a scorcher. We can get the sun."

"Sure," I said.

And right there in the locker room, he took hold of me and gave me the happiest kiss I'd ever felt, a promise of things to come, oblivious of the guy across from us who was getting out of his khakis.

***

HE TOOK a joint out of his right pocket and a Zippo out of his left and we shared the smoke as we walked arm in arm on Christopher Street toward the river. We passed the Theater de Lys where The Three Penny Opera was still playing, and saw Lotte Lenya, with orange hair, going in, a cigarette in one hand, a Styrofoam container of coffee in the other.

"What do you do?" I asked Brian as we passed One Fifty Two, where Reich's Orgone Institute Press had been located before the Feds busted him and combusted all his books a little north of us on the Gansevoort Pier.

"I'm getting a doctorate in Economics and Poly Sci. Right now I play the piano in a bar. You?"

"I'm writing a doctoral thesis, in psychology."

He leaned over and bit me on the neck. My cock began to dance.

"You'll never figure me out," he said.

"I don't want to," I said. "I want to figure you in."

***

ON THE pier we stripped down to our jocks and lay in the sun. He gently traced indecipherable patterns on my chest and kissed my nipples and filled my mouth with his tongue. It was heavenly.

"I like when you're passive," he said, gazing into my eyes and caressing my cheek. "I can tell how hot you are."

The sky was an intense azure above us, the sun ablaze with happiness. I felt like the end of the world had come, that history had reached its climax, that the rest of my life needed to be the extension of this minute.

We sat gazing into each other's eyes.

"I'm afraid," I said.

"Of what?" he said.

"That this will end," I said.

"It will," he said, "and it won't."

I waited.

"It's inside you forever."

"But longing for it afterwards..."

"...is a mistake." And then he kissed me.

"Come on," he said, getting to his feet and lifting me to mine.

At Sheridan Square he said he had to go.

I panicked quietly, but only said. "Will we see each other again?"

"There's a midnight screening of *Limelight* at the Bleecker Street tomorrow. I'm free. Meet me in front at quarter to."

"Ok," I said.

"I gotta run," he said, "I work tonight." He gave me a quick kiss on the lips. Then, throwing out his arm, seductively, he camped, "Till then."

And then he was gone.

I knew his name was Brian; that's all. Not his phone number, not his address, not the bar where he played.

I was elated. But something inside me wondered for how long.

***

BRIAN WAS on the corner when I got to the Bleecker Street Theater. It had cooled off and he was wearing jeans, a white shirt with frills, half unbuttoned, suede moccasins without socks and a tuxedo jacket with a rounded midnight blue satin lapel.

Down Bleecker, right onto MacDougal, left onto West 3rd, across Sixth Avenue, north from the Waverly, west on 4th a bit, then left onto Jones Street, arms round each other after the movie in the still night overhung with the sliver crescent of a silver moon in a clear sky. Lust made our feet unstable. His apartment was in a tall old tenement whose gray marble steps were worn down by a century of trodding.

By candle light we smoked a joint and I slid down out of his arms to his feet and knelt before him and began to lick his ankles until he took me by the hair, guided me up, kissed me deep inside my mouth with his tongue, unbuttoned my shirt and gazed at my bare chest. Then he undid my belt, unbuttoned my jeans and I stood before him naked, hard-cocked and glassy-eyed.

"I'm going to hypnotize you," he said, "taking hold of my nipples, "and turn you into my slave. Do you want to be my slave?"

"I want to be your slave," I said, shivering as a current of electricity shot through me.

"Look into the candle flame," he said, and slowly started drawing me into his orbit.

I don't know if he succeeded in actually hypnotizing me. I certainly was willing, and I couldn't tell the difference between pretending and the real thing.

And, finally, it didn't matter, because, I thought, Brian was the real thing.

***

BEING THE real thing is different from being a permanent thing. In fact, I've come to think that the permanent thing never can be the real thing. The permanent thing is stuck too much in accommodations and compromises, and now I think that, on the whole, that's a good thing. I didn't think so then. I believed in phosphorescent intensity, in the drama of overwhelming illumination.

Oh how I wanted him, and every time we got together and he wanted me the earth spun on its axis and the constellations in heaven glowed into explosion.

It was my unease, my doubt, my insecurity, my fear that there would be no next time that made that glorious joy and overwhelming excitement each time there was a next time.

***

EVERYONE KNEW McGovern would lose, yet it came as a shock when he did, because our hearts were young and we believed that the impossible could happen, that reversals were possible, that water might gush out of a rock and the heart might open to gentleness. Suddenly we felt horribly isolated, terribly alone in a dark eternal moment.

For Brian it was a turning point. We spent election night in my apartment on Bedford Street gazing into each other's eyes, cradled in each other's arms. In the morning, he smiled at me with all his soul. Perhaps he even left his soul with me through that smile, for it is an expression of his I never see on television or in the news photos of him now, but it was so much a part of him then.

Now his expressions more closely resemble the three fundamental ones in the president's repertoire of facial expressions: the smirk, the sneer, and the snarl. Each, on a face still handsome, has a peculiar although insidious and even frightening but inescapable charm.

Brian said -- that morning in November 1972 -- after his soul's smile fell from his face, "It's never going to be the same again. Remember, I love you." And he kissed me again. Solemnity like a sudden wind blew over his face. He caressed my cheek and looked at me...was it with disappearing eyes? I could find no sure reason for it, but a shiver of uneasiness, of foreboding, coursed through me and was just as quickly gone as he repeated, "Remember," when he turned back momentarily as he descended the stairs.

***

WHEN I stopped by Crazy Benny's Friday night to hear him play and have a drink with him at the bar before we went home to his place or mine as we did every Friday night, he was distant, hardly even polite, distant, and his focus was on a preppy-looking guy with a military haircut in a double breasted blue jacket with gold buttons, chino slacks, white buck shoes, a burgundy foulard tucked inside his open-collared television blue oxford shirt, and horn-rimmed glasses.

Rather stiffly Brian introduced me to "Dean" as "a Friday night regular," which I was, but not in the sense he was using the term now. And then he excused himself as if he were just talking to a fan, and I saw a look on his face I'd never seen before that made it impossible to say anything more, because even though he was Brian, he wasn't, so whatever I would say would appear unhinged from anything real. He wasn't the guy who kissed me or had a smattering of love for me, so how could I remind him of what had become another man's kisses? It was crazy.

They sat at a table in the back and ordered cognac. Dean was leaning in across the small table, and talking with a quiet intensity, and Brian was mesmerized by his gaze. I stayed at the bar, had a beer to try to get some perspective, took a few swallows, but found my throat was closed. I left it three-quarters unfinished and quit the place. I walked home in the chilly November night unable to focus my thoughts or get a read on my feelings.

***

BRIAN DIDN'T answer his phone for a few days, and after that there was a recorded announcement informing me (or anyone who called) that the line was no longer in service. Brian wasn't playing at Crazy Benny's anymore, either, and when I asked Alan, one of my favorite bartenders, he said that Brian had just stopped showing up.

"Didn't even pick up his last paycheck."

When I inquired at NYU, I found out Brian had moved out of the city and transferred to George Mason in Virginia.

I guess when Brian had tried to hypnotize me, he hadn't really succeeded. I wasn't hung up on him. He went away. He faded away. I got my degree. I've had lots of lovers and one or two for keeps. I have a good practice, and I'm proud to say I've also been in jail a few times for non-violent civil disobedience in the cause of raising consciousness on issues of peace, racial and economic justice, and sexual liberation. The times may seem bleak, but I recognize lots of fellow travelers, and most of them aren't lonesome.

As for Brian, when I see him on television now among the neo-conservative cabal or with the president at a press conference or on Meet the Press defending one indefensible policy or another, rather than being dispirited by the sight of a good looking guy defending brutal atrocities and mesmerizing the Americans with ideological trigger phrases, I see the skull beneath the skin. I know, even if he doesn't, that somewhere inside him, buried deep, he's grinning, not smirking or snarling, stripped of his shirt and making love to some guy on a hot summer afternoon under the West Side Highway in the back of a truck. I remember.

If only he could.

End of the 3rd book

FLUENCY
of the
Heart

Gideon Elliot

Fluency of the Heart

I had not slept for I could not tell you how long. I mean real sleep -- deep, seamless, dreamless sleep. I mean the kind of sleep that is without the disturbed images of inverted and inside-out consciousness, the images that turbulate on a non-existent, four-dimensional screen, images that come to life in some amorphous medium that is located somewhere beyond the boundaries of the space and time that I think I occupy. This perversely reconstructed reality provides me illusory escape in the five or ten minute hypnogogic episodes that I succumb to every now and then, but no respite.

I was living on honey-heavy Turkish coffee, vitamin B, and fresh orange juice from the juice bar down the block. I was hyper. My father used to call it speeding. My mind was fast, but sharp, and clear, and my body was like a knife. My eyes pierced anything they looked at.

"Man, you go on like this," Denny said from behind the bar as he crushed some blood oranges in some high-tech chromium juicer he used, "and you ain't gonna be alive in six weeks."

"Wanna bet?"

"How much?" he said with a wink.

"You get to fuck me."

"If I win?"

"No, if you win I'm dead, and I didn't think even you were that kinky."

"So if I lose I get to fuck you?"

"Right."

"And if I win?"

"You're outta luck?"

"Deal," he said.

It wasn't really a joke. He was fixated on it, fucking me. Every time we got together, he always finally got around to asking.

"Isn't this good enough?" I'd say taking him by his cock and kissing him on the lips.

He got hard as hell in my hand and his breath ran away from him.

"More than enough."

But it was not enough. Enough was owning me.

"But I gotta warn you," I said, slapping an old Susan Anthony on the counter as he handed me the juice, "even if you get to fuck me, which I'm perfectly confident you will, you're not going to own me."

"You're probably right," he said, "but I still want to feel what it'll be like to fuck you."

"I guarantee you'll like it," I said.

The place was not empty. But it didn't matter. We touched our lips together over the counter and I split with a wink.

***

TUESDAY NIGHT, I didn't sleep, either. But that was for the best. I finished my column and decided I'd bring it over to the paper myself instead of e-mailing it.

The night was balmy. The streets were nearly deserted. I walked down to West Street and turned right. The paper's editorial offices were in the twenties. Frank buzzed me in.

"It's slow tonight," he said, "Good to see you."

"You look like shit," I said, but it was not an insult.

"We don't get much sleep since the baby came," he said.

"How is May?" I said.

"She's wonderful," he said. "Exhausted, but she thrives on it."

"And the kid?"

"Ah," Frank said. "You're the one who can do things with words. Me, I wish my heart was more fluent in English so I could express how I feel."

"That ain't bad," I said.

"I read it in a story on the AP wire. A guy who's refusing to go to Iraq, his father said it about him to express how proud he was."

"It's good," I said.

"But what are you doing up at this hour?"

"With no new baby as an excuse, huh?" I said.

"Yeah," he said.

"I got a lot of old babies who keep me up."

"That and all the Turkish coffee you drink."

"You know me, Al."

"You still writing about S&M?" Frank said, glancing quickly at my copy.

"Uh huh."

"Be careful, Max."

"Careful?"

"Some of these guys are very serious about their games. They're like secret ceremonies, old mysteries. They need the darkness to thrive. They don't like reporters."

"You shall know the truth and the truth shall make you..."

"Scared! Especially when you start making connections, life can get very short."

"Jeez, Frank, you're the second person tonight who's talked to me about death."

"Just be careful, Max."

"I'm glad Chekhov isn't writing this story."

"How do you know he isn't?"

"Because he's dead."

***

IT WAS after one when I left with Frank, who turned the place over to Richard, who got off at nine the next morning. Frank headed down to the Village on West Street. I headed east into Chelsea where the bars were still open. I stopped into Crazy Benny's first, figuring I'd have a brandy and find out from Ezra, the bar guy there, if he'd heard anything it would be worth it to me to know.

It wasn't exactly packed, but for that hour on a Wednesday morning, nearly two a.m., there was a good size crowd.

"It's been relatively quiet," Ezra said. "If you want heavy leather and squealing pig stuff, you still have to go to Thirteenth Street, a block from the water, a place called The Troth."

We spoke and I looked around.

"He's pretty," I said.

"That's Martin," Ezra said. "The twink with him is called Domino because he falls easy but his name's really Tim."

Martin was actually more than pretty. He was exquisite, fine, solid, delicate, and masculine all at once. Tim was diaphanous springtime personified.

Martin stood beside the bar, nearly six feet, tall, lean and graceful as a panther. As subtle, too, and as beautiful, and as capricious, now a sweet cat and now a dangerous one. His eyes were soft and softly burning. Something in them let you know they could express defiance as well as desire.

He touched his glass to the one the young white kid, not yet twenty, Tim, tilted towards him and smiled. He was in a mellow mood, casting a gentle spell all around.

"Oh, you don't know how I want you," Martin whispered huskily, yes, huskily, for he was loose and right with alcohol. "Everything down there is quivering for you."

"You think I don't know what it's like," Tim answered. "It makes the way you move so sexy," he said, lithe like a panther. It sends a shock and a current through me."

"Like a black panther," Martin said, pressing one palm against the side of Tim's bare waist.

With the index finger of his other hand he traced the blue-black length of the asp tattooed on Tim's chest. He stopped at the asp's head, which covered a nipple and pinched it, hard. It felt to Tim as if the asp were biting. He gasped.

"That's only the beginning," Martin said.

"I hope so," Tim said, sucking in a breath and biting his teeth together.

***

FIVE OF them were piled in an old Chrysler across the street from the bar, waiting for excitement, waiting for trouble.

"How come they let niggers in there?"

"He ain't a nigger. He's an A-rab."

"Same difference."

"Just the same he ought to know he ain't welcome on this street."

They trembled as they spoke and passed around a bottle of Jack Daniels. They thought it was anger that made them shake. But it was the thrill of being in each other's company and being of one mind.

"Faggots! One's a nigger and both of 'em are faggots. Look at 'em."

Martin and Tim walked away from the bar's entrance towards the subway, trying to steer clear of trouble.

"Hey! Not so fast," Barron, sitting behind the wheel, called to them. And he released the emergency brake, because that was the only brake that worked, and let the car crawl down the street beside Martin and Tim. There was no traffic otherwise. The street was empty except for Martin and Tim, and the guys in the car stalked them slowly. The hulking car rolled and sent out a wave of threat.

Martin put his arm around Tim as they walked. Tim leaned into him.Martin's bare arm was hard and muscled and warm against his flesh. He held Tim softly, oh so softly. And Tim was hard for him even though he was scared.

"At a time like this," Martin said quietly and steadily, "you have to know who you are no matter what you look like. There's a difference, and it matters that you remember that."

"You want to get in the car and give us a good time, too, jungle boy?" one of the punks with a shaved head called out of a back window.

Hooting and shouting, they were afraid of what they wanted and wanted what they were afraid of. They lived in fear and brought fear with them everywhere they went.

Now, Martin, not letting go of Tim, the kid told me when I spoke to him at the morgue, turned and faced them. The car stopped.

"The nigger fag is gonna make a speech," Barron, a punk in the back sneered. "I have a dream. A wet dream!"

Barron pulled up the emergency brake, and the car lurched to a stop, and a woosh of dirty exhaust smoked out of the tail pipe.

"Why don't you guys look for other amusement?" Martin said.

"You know, murders can begin this way," someone inside the car yelled.

"Yours, nigger," another cried.

And then there was the flash of a gun and the report of a shot and the screech of the engine as Barron released the emergency brake and gunned it out of there.

Martin lay on the ground and Tim was holding him, his head, his chest. He knew Martin was dead and he was numb.

Martin, in fact, was dead when I saw the body in the morgue, but Tim was not. And, ashamed as I ought to be to write this, he was ravishing when I saw him all in black, black turtle neck, fitted black velvet suit, black boots, and his skin, transparent, clear, luminous, delicate. The boy was an incarnation of fragility.

"It means nothing that they caught them," he said. "It does not bring Martin back to life."

"And it does not bring you back to life, either," I said.

"No," he said. He understood what I meant.

"But wait," I said. "Give it time. Desire will be reborn and it will grow."

"I wonder if I want it to," he said. "If it does, it will feel like betrayal."

"No," I said. "Living without desire is betrayal."

"Perhaps," he said.

I gave him my card.

"Call me whenever. Keep in touch. Let me know how you are getting on."

He walked over to the place on Perry Street that he shared with his sister.

I took a cab east.

***

DENNY WAS gentle with me, not because I was a bottom virgin. I wasn't. But my soul was still sensitive and I lived with the ache of what had happened.

When we heard the shot, Ezra looked at me.

"That ain't a truck backfiring," I said.

I saw Tim hunched over Martin's body, and I put my arm around him and helped him up.

Ezra touched Martin's chest.

"The man is dead."

"What happened?" I asked Tim. "I know it's hard but it's important you tell us, the quicker the better if we're gonna catch them."

Ezra called 911 on his cell phone and six squad cars, lights turning, sirens blaring were there before he snapped it shut.

I held Tim, my arm around him as he told the cops what happened and the direction the car went off in.

"Does he have to go down to the precinct house?" I asked McCreedy of the Sixth.

He shook his head kindly.

"You can stay with me tonight," I said.

"Ok," Tim said.

"I'll give you a ride," McCreedy said. He knew where I lived. No one else knew it, but we'd seen each other a couple of times. He'd even slept over.

"If this is what loosing feels like," Denny said, kissing me sweetly on the lips.

"No, Denny, this is not what loosing feels like," I said opening to him like a melancholy gardenia.

I held him around the neck tight and raised myself up and kissed him as I felt him slowly taking me all the way inside him, even though it was really the other way around. I opened to him and felt him touch me in another country beyond the borders where I lived, and I smiled at him and thanked him as he sweetly fucked me.

"I didn't expect that kind of sentiment from you," he said as he gently stroked me and took me back into the world where I wasn't sure I wanted to go.

"I hardly knew him," Tim said, looking softly into my eyes, reciprocating my gaze.

"I'd met him that night. It might have gone nowhere, where things like that usually go after the first night, but what happened made it get stuck in me. Or it made me get stuck, right in the middle of love. It did not have the chance to die. What a weird thing. Because he died, the love did not have a chance to die."

"It's painful," I said.

"Like what a pain is supposed to feel like in an amputated leg."

I took him in my arms and pressed him to me and gently kissed his delicate temple.

"Thanks," he said, his body yielding to exhaustion.

Beyond us the Hudson River slowly flowed and the sky rose forever like nothing had happened.

End of the 4th book

On The Cusp

Gideon Elliot

On the Cusp

You ask what am I muttering, stupefied.
It is a prayer of thanks
that there is such a thing
as you in the world there.

Paul Goodman, "Such Beauty as Hurts to Behold"

***

HE HELD himself more proudly than anyone else I had ever seen and was nevertheless an open and winning person. He had a smile that went deep and looks that were worth looking at. There was gentleness to his intelligence, curiosity in his gaze, an awareness that other people existed in his conversation and behavior. His pride was simply animal awareness of animal health. He was the embodiment of good spirits.

He was on the swimming team, so his body was smooth and his head was shaven nearly hairless. But it only brought out the beauty of his face.

I looked at him every chance I could get and went to watch the swim meets just to see him in his little black speedo bikini diving into the pale clear blue water that even in the bleachers smelled of chlorine. I daydreamed about him all the time.

That made me feel really small, to be daydreaming about a guy, making him a character in my fantasies. That was pathetic. I would have been ashamed if anyone knew, but it, nevertheless, really excited me to think of him, to picture him, to imagine being pals with him. He was a puppet in my theater of hopeless longing.

I was beyond desiring him. I was obsessed with, possessed by my fantasy of, him.

***

I WALKED to school every day by myself, and it was a time for major daydreaming.

His name was David, not Brian, or Red, or Rich, but David. Like there was a world of thought in his head. Me, I knew I was filling up my head with movies, with wishes, with fantasies of having power and being loved. I knew that my intelligence would get stopped at a border that other people could get across. I knew that I slouched when I walked, that in gym I got worn out before I got excited. David lived in a world I envied. He wasn't blocked by boundaries, by weakness, by uncertainty.

I knew his house; I passed it every morning passing along the wide suburban street. There were trees everywhere along the street, extending branches to meet the branches of trees on the other side of the street. Arches formed a perfect world for walking through the mind.

His house was a small Tudor mansion. I'd seen him enter and leave several times, and I imagined there were wonders inside, luxurious furniture, gorgeous carpets, glamorous clothes in walk-in closets, bathrooms like Turkish baths, and rooms for parties where great intimacies occurred.

***

IF YOU weren't alive and at least in your early teens in the late nineteen-fifties, you missed something. It was a time when marvellous cultural changes were taking place, and it was clear that they were. Signs of an old way cracking and a new one establishing itself were everywhere. Changes in conventional consciousness, in patterns of behavior and thought, in values, in ways of dressing, appeared in every quarter.

I started hanging around Greenwich Village, and it was down in the Village, not in Forest Hills, that I met David and found out who he really was.

I was walking through Washington Square Park, the old, woodsy Washington Square Park with enclosed umbrageous alleys that existed before Bob Nichols redesigned it, suburbanized it, invited the barrenness that would overwhelm its charm in the early sixties. It was an overcast day in November with brittle leaves carpeting the ground. It felt like it was going to snow.

There was David sitting on a park bench beside a lamppost. He was smoking a pipe, wearing an Ezra Pound fedora, and writing in a notebook.

Perhaps the shock of recognizing him that I experienced set up a disturbance in him and broke his concentration, signaling something was around that needed to be noticed.

For whatever reason, he looked up, saw me, and I was surprised when he said hello using my name.

Of course, he knew it, he said, when I asked him how he knew my name. He saw me nearly every day after eighth period in the library where I worked, and he often heard Mrs. Ferguson, the head librarian, use it.

So he had noticed me. I hadn't thought that he had all the times I'd noticed him.

"Gray," he said, rising from the bench, waving his hand at the sky. "Snow."

"I never thought I'd see you here," I said before I had the sense not to.

"Why not?"

I was stupidly without an answer.

"I like to come down here and write," he said, coming to my rescue. "There's a feeling around here that I like. I know; you figured I was a dumb-ass jock."

I tried to deny it, but he started rough-housing with me. "Maybe a wrestler," he said, "who could get you in a head lock."

I squirmed and he finally released me, pressing a kiss like lightening upon the back of my neck, and saying into my ear before loosening his hold, "See, I know you better than you know me."

I was entirely at a loss. Was he making fun of me?

"Do you drink coffee?" he asked. "Do you wanna go have a coffee?" It was friendly.

"Sure," I said.

We crossed out of the park onto University Place, and stopped to read the plaque commemorating the deaths of the sewing machine girls in the 1911 Triangle fire.

"Do you know about that?"

I didn't, and I said so, and he described the conditions that people worked under when they could be locked in a room from morning till night. He told me about how a fire had started and how the girls had no way out of the burning building except by jumping out the windows.

"And working conditions like that still are common, even in America," he said.

He told me his dad was a labor lawyer and that he had plans to be one, too, but sometimes he thought he just wanted to be a poet and lead a bohemian life.

"I want to explore consciousness, the process of being aware, independent of what you're aware of."

"How you see things," I suggested.

"Or how the things you see aren't really there, and things that you can't see are."

And then without missing a beat the rhythm of his speech changed. His face was bright. His voice was light. Intensity was in his eyes.

***

WE SAT for hours in the Figaro, it began to snow, and if I wasn't in love with him already, I fell in love with him then.

It was after ten when we left the Figaro.

David had keys to a friend's apartment at number fifty on MacDougal, and he was staying there tonight because Michael was visiting his girlfriend who lived in Trenton where she went to school. He asked me if I wanted to sleep over.

It was five flights up. You entered a kitchen and there were several small rooms off it.

It was hot in the apartment from steam heat, and David took off his shirt and told me to take off mine, too. So I did.

"Not bad," David said. "You could pass for a jock, too, if you didn't slouch, and if you didn't wear your pants so high.

"Me?" I said. "I'm too skinny."

He opened a closet in the bedroom, pulled out a pair of jeans and told me to try them on.

I blushed. I was shaking. I tried to look at David like nothing was on my mind, but all I wanted to do was touch him.

"Come on," he said.

So I stripped, but when he saw my baggy boxers, he laughed.

"I don't ever want to see you wearing such a monstrosity again. Try these," he said, giving me a pair of black bikini briefs that I had looked at many times with longing as I daydreamed in front of the window of The Shed House on West Fourth Street.

I went into the bathroom to change. I felt nervously erotic when I emerged.

"You want to play a game?" He said.

"Sure," I said, hoping maybe it would relieve some of the tension I felt in trying to fight off obsessive feelings of desire.

"Ok," he said. "Let's see who can not touch the other one longer."

I looked at him puzzled.

"That way we can hang out all night and do nothing interesting."

And then I got it, but before I could say anything, David leaned over and took my nipples between his thumbs and forefingers and kissed me on the lips and said, "I guess I lose."

I looked at him and a light came on in his eyes and I fell into his arms and was devoured by his kisses, and twisted under him, transformed by his grace into something graceful myself.

In the morning, the transformation was still there. There was a circle of gold surrounding us.

We walked through Greenwich Village in the very early morning, astonished by what had happened.

But nothing really was important, because we had done something to each other that made us gravitate towards each other in the flesh. And for us, then, that became a very serious argument for the legitimacy of our passion.

Queer, I was queer. I should care. I was rhapsodic. I wanted everyone to know I had given myself to David. The definition of heaven was that he wanted me.

The snow began again to tumble through the sky. We wanted to be back in the apartment, and we left the snowy streets of Sixth Avenue for an old Village tenement and a bed, candlelight, a joint and each other. The world was changing, and we were the change.

Creator spirit, come.

THE END

WANT FREE COPIES OF MY BOOKS?
Just visit my blog and download free copies of my books:
http://gideon-elliot.awesomeauthors.org/gideon-elliot/

Here is a sample from another story you may enjoy:

6-BOOK BOX SET

My Fair
MASTER

Gay Erotic Romance
GIDEON ELLIOT

In Antibes, just outside the walls of the old city, on the rue de Recherche, where boys lean against the wall wearing hardly more than their dark summer tans and wait for free-spending tourists to notice them, there's an absinthe bar in the basement of a shop that sells gourmet olive oil, scented vinegar, hand-crafted kitchen implements, mixed herbs, exotic pastas, and fancy soap during the day mostly to Americans and Germans who have a particular fondness for their kitchens and their bathrooms and the money to indulge it.

Looking like a van Gogh in yellow, blue, olive, and red, the assomoir is open after the shop upstairs has long been shut. Patrons come and leave through an ill-lit side entrance negotiating a flight of steep and twisting wooden steps. The pale and dirty stucco walls are coated with a red stain cast by the bare exit bulb stuck in the ceiling.

It is a quiet place with marble table tops and amber light bulbs. Water carafes with little spigots stand on chrome feet at the center of the tables. Sometimes some of the boys from outside lean against the bar nursing a drink and look blank, waiting for something to happen. I had taken to hanging out there nearly every night, either passing through just for one drink at the bar, or sometimes settling at one of the round tables to write or to sketch. Every now and then I'd gaze at the boys, admiring their youth, but since I never would consent to be a paying customer, none of them had eyes for me. And all I was left with was to wonder at their unreflecting inwardness.

As I was about to leave one evening in early August, hoping to take a walk along the ramparts overlooking the blue Mediterranean before complete nightfall, a young American, a good looking sunned and tousle-haired boy of around nineteen with sparkling, questing, needy eyes asked if he could sit down at my table.

"Sure," I said.

"I've seen you several times before this," he said, fastening his gaze upon me and catching mine in his.

I looked him over to see if I could recognize him, but had no recollection of having seen him before and was quite certain, given his good looks and lean but well-wrought frame apparent under his loose-hanging striped boatman shirt and faded jeans, that I would have if I had.

He smiled showing perfect teeth.

"You're not one of them," I said.

"What?"

"You're not one of the beach boys that hang around the street at night."

"No," he said. "I'm not."

"I can tell," I said.

"How?" he asked smiling. "By my eyes?"

"No," I said. "By the loose hang of your clothes."

He blushed.

"Who are you?" I said.

He told me his name.

"I've never seen you here before," I said. But I recognized his name. "Your father," I began, but he interrupted me.

"Yes," he said, and I knew all I needed to know and from politeness moved quickly away from the subject.

"Have we met?" I asked.

"I don't expect you'd have noticed me," he said modestly. "The last time I saw you, it was at the Picasso museum and you were totally absorbed by the de Stael exhibition. A few days before that, I saw you with a German boy having coffee in a café above the beach."

I winced. I remembered him.

He blushed when he added, "the only thing I think you could see was his eyes. You both were gazing into each other's eyes to the exclusion of everything else."

"It happens," I said, "when I get lucky," I added, not without irony as we continued to mirror each other's gaze.

He registered the ambiguity but proceeded without letting it sabotage him.

"I want it to happen to me," he said, and blushed again, nevertheless
looking straight at me.

"You do?" I said.

"With you," he said.

"With me," I said, quizzically.

"Yes," he said, determined not to be put off.

"Have you ever had absinthe?"

"I've only read about it," he said, shaking his head.

"Laurent," I said to the barman, signaling for a glass of La Muse Verte for the boy and a refill for me.

He brought them and I added water to each.

"You can put sugar in if you like," I said, "but I don't."

"Then I won't either," he said." I want to do things the way you do."

I looked at him.

"I have a sixth sense," he said, as we tilted our glasses towards each other, and our eyes began their slow embrace.

"I want you to make me your boy," he said. "I want to belong to you."

"Do you know what that means?" I said.

"I think I do," he said, "and I want to know how it feels." His voice was deep and sweet and slow.

I couldn't tell who was taking control of whom as we gazed into each other's eyes.

"Have you ever made love to a man?" I asked.

"No," he answered.

"Do you want to?"

"If the man is you," he said.

If you enjoyed this sample then look for **My Fair Master**.

Also by this Author

From the Author

WANT FREE COPIES OF MY BOOKS?

Just visit my blog and download free copies of my books:

http://gideon-elliot.awesomeauthors.org/gideon-elliot/

Check my page on Amazon and my blog for Updates and interesting info.

Author Central - http://www.amazon.com/Gideon-Elliot/e/B00DUYBEQC

If you enjoyed any of my books then please share the love and click like on my books in Amazon.

If you write me a review and send me an email I will send you a free book, or many.
(Just know that these emails are filtered by my publisher.)

Good news is always welcome.

One Last Thing, For Kindle Readers...

When you turn the page, Kindle will give you the opportunity to rate this book and share your thoughts on Facebook and Twitter. If you enjoyed my writings, would you please take a few seconds to let your friends know about it? Because... when they enjoy they will be grateful to you and so will I.

Thank You!

Gideon Elliot
gideon_elliot@awesomeauthors.org

About the Author

Gideon Elliot was born in 1981 in Wichita, Kansas.

He grew up in San Francisco and spends the greater part of the year, now, on one of the Cyclades Islands in Greece where he runs a jazz café, paints, writes poetry, and swims.

He has a small apartment in Greenwich Village, where he stays from the middle of November to the end of April and, during those months, manages an erotic men's clothing shop. He began writing erotic fiction at the age of fifteen.

You may also like the books by these authors:

DEXTER CHASE

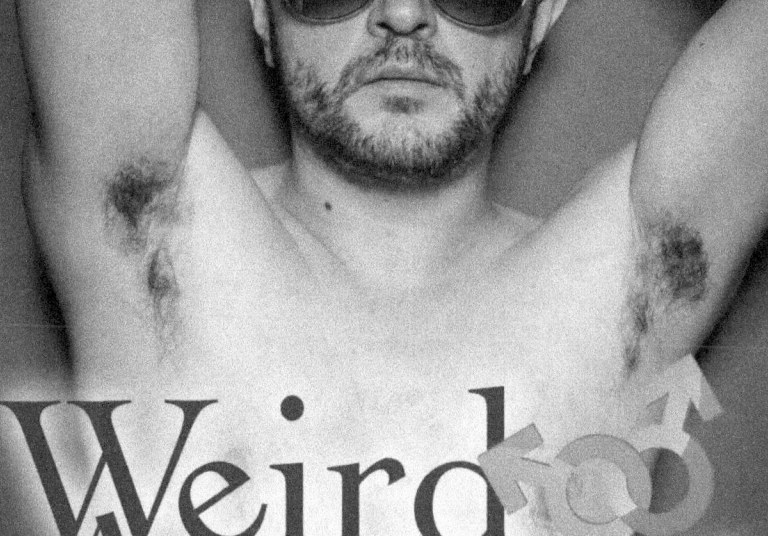

Weird Arrangement

Gay Domination and Submission

Teaching senior year economics at the only senior high in the town gave him so much pleasure. He also headed the school debating team as he had done in college. Last week they had debated Darwin's theory of evolution which in this southern Baptist County was considered heresy and worse.

Satisfied with his appearance, Robb walked back to his bedroom and dressed carefully as always. Button-down dress shirt, close fitting chinos, Gucci loafers, thin gold dress watch and he was ready to take on the world. Mr. Neat and Careful would sum up Robb perfectly. He had been an athlete through school and college, keeping in perfect shape and condition for his sport. Now he worked out in the school gym most days to maintain that shape or in his home gym. Robb was a very closeted gay and released all the pent up needs in the gym. He scoped out the senior boys that worked out after school as well, discretely of course. He was popular with them and was considered a nice guy, if a little uptight. The few gay ones lusted after him as well but were also deep in the closet. Home for a shower and a long session masturbating, thinking about the sexiest boys he had seen that day. He could watch them strip for showers but he always carried that out at home.

His final action before leaving for school was a healthy breakfast with black coffee.

Robb drove his BMW drop head coupe with total pleasure and pulled into the staff car park at precisely 0845. Electric hood up, car locked, he was in the staff room at 0850, checking his schedule and collecting his lesson plans for the morning. He was sat at his desk by 0855 and watched the students enter and sit down in an orderly fashion completed by 0900.

"Good morning, everyone."

The reply always pleased him. He didn't like these 18-year-olds calling him 'sir', so he smiled as he heard, "Good morning, Mr. Talbot."

Most other teachers put up with a noisy start to their day but Robb had made it clear that noise meant demerits, besides, most of his classes liked his no-nonsense approach and his high standards of lecturing.

"This morning we are going to continue our study of Adam Smith."

Books were opened at the proper page and they all settled in to listen to Robb. He was well into the discussion when the door opened and two slave police walked in. Never one to tolerate interruptions to his class, Robb bridled and told the two men to wait outside until the class was finished.

"Are you Mr. Robb Talbot?"

"Yes, of course I am, now please leave, you are interrupting my lesson."

The obvious leader of the two policemen opened a paper and read.

"At a court hearing held in this county at 0700 this morning evidence was produced showing that you preached heresy at a debating society meeting held in this school last week. The recorded session made it unnecessary for the judge to call you. You are condemned by your own words. The verdict is 'slavery for life' and we are here to execute that order. Now, remove all of your clothes, Slave."

The class let out a uniform gasp of shock and Robb spluttered out a, "Don't be ridiculous, I'm not undressing for you."

The Taser hit him as he finished and he was writhing on the floor. When he recovered he stood up again facing the police.

"You can take your clothes off, Slave, or we can do it for you."

If you enjoyed this sample then look for <u>Weird Arrangement</u>.

GAY ROMANCE EROTICA

FIRSTLOVE

DICKPARKER

The next day, Friday was game day. Austin hadn't practiced enough so he could suit up for the game, so he stood on the sidelines with me and the coaches and other managers. He and I walked the edge of the field watching the game and talked. It was the most fun I'd had at a game in all of my high school years. We lost.

I had all the equipment put away and towels picked up and Austin hung around and waited for me.

"How 'bout getting a burger or something?" he asked.

"I don't have any money."

"Ah'll buy."

"I can't ask you to pay my way, Austin. It's nice enough that you're friendly with me."

He put his hands on my shoulders and looked me right in the eyes.

"Listen, little man. Ah'm not askin ya'll cause I feel sorry for you. Ah'm askin ya'll cause Ah like ya'll."

I looked into his beautiful brown eyes and at his handsome face and I had all I could do to keep from kissing him. He grinned at me and winked.

"So?"

"Okay. Can we stop at my house so I can tell Gram?"

"No problem."

We stopped and I invited him in to meet my Grandma. She was very happy to meet him. I knew it was because I finally had a friend. He was very polite with her.

"She's a lovely lady," he said as we drove away.

"I'm so glad I have her. If it wouldn't have been for her I'd have been in foster care."

"So what do you feel like eating?" he asked.

"I'm good for anything."

We went to a pizza place.

There were a lot of kids from school there. Some stopped by and said hi to Austin. Several girls stopped and flirted with him.

"The girls think you're hot," I said.

"Yeah, well there you go."

"Did you have a girlfriend back home?"

"Not really. I kind of played the field."

I nodded.

"How 'bout you, Ronan? You ever had a girlfriend?"

I shook my head.

"Ever kiss a girl?"

"Other than my Grandma?"

He grinned.

"Yeah."

"Nope."

"So you never had sex."

"You mean with someone else?"

He burst out laughing. He'd just taken a drink of coke and spit it all over the table. He began choking and I slapped him on the back.

"Damn ya'll."

"Sorry. I didn't mean to make you choke."

"It's okay. So ya'll just pull on yer willie?"

"Yeah I guess. All guys do, don't they?"

"Hell yeah. Ma peter is ma best friend."

We laughed some more, but in my mind I had a picture of him naked and jacking off.

"Ya'll a squirter or a dribbler?"

"It depends. Sometimes I squirt."

He ruffled my hair.

"Ah like ya'll, Ronan."

"I like you too."

He took me home and we stopped in the street.

"What ya'll doin tomorrow?"

"Nothing."

"Wanta go fishin?"

"I've never been fishing. I don't have a pole or anything."

"Ya'll never been fishin? Holy shit. Ya'll want to try it?"

"Sure."

"How bout we go and fish and camp out and stay overnight?"

"Really? Do you have a tent and stuff?"

"Ah got everything."

"I'd have to ask Grandma."

"Go run in and ask her."

I ran in and Grandma was happy that I was going. I ran back out and told him I could go.

"What do I need to bring?"

"Just bring some extra clothes and ya'll's tooth brush. I got everything else we need."

We left it that he'd pick me up at nine in the morning. I was so excited that I jumped up in the truck and wrapped my arms around him and hugged him. He hugged me back and smiled at me when I let go.

"See ya'll tomorrow, my friend."

I was so excited I couldn't sleep. I lay in my bed thinking about Austin. I pictured his face and his cap and hair. Then I pictured his chest and stomach and then his cock and balls. God, he was perfect.

"What the hell does he see in me?" I asked myself.

I lay there thinking of how his cock looked hanging there swinging back and forth. I wondered how big it got when it got hard. I guessed that it had a little hook to the left just from the way it hung. I wondered what it looked like with the skin back off the head.

My own cock got hard. I rubbed it and played with my balls. There was no way I was going to sleep without jacking off. I grabbed a pair of socks and held them in one hand while I jacked with the other. I closed my eyes and pictured Austin. He was jacking off too and he was grinning at me. I began squirting and shot cum up in the air.

Then I lay there breathing hard. Boy he asked me if I was a squirter or a dribbler. I bet he didn't think I'd picture him and be a shooter.

Gram made cookies and I took a bag of them with me when Austin picked me up. She waved from the front porch.

"It's gonna be a great weekend. I asked a friend of my Dad and he told me about this lake near here. He said the fishing is good and it's nice and clean so we can swim too."

"I didn't bring a swimming suit," I said.

He grinned.

"We don't need no swimming suit."

Oh boy.

We stopped and got me a fishing license and some worms. Then we drove to the lake. We found a nice campsite near the water and there weren't any other campers near us. It was late in the season and many had put their stuff away for the year.

We set up the tent. It was small but with plenty of room for two sleeping bags. Then we gathered some wood and got everything ready for the night. Austin took off his shirts and shoes. He only had on shorts.

"Why don't ya'll get some sun?"

"Oh I'm not full of muscles like you, Austin."

"Oh come on. Ah'm the only what will see ya'll."

I felt skinny and weak next to him. I took off my shoes and socks and then pulled my shirt off. He smiled.

"Ya'll look nice, Ronan. Yer small but very nicely put together."

He moved close to me and ran his hand over my chest. He touched my nipples. Then he rubbed over my belly.

"Yer nice and firm. With a little work, ya'll can get a good build."

"Like you?'

He nodded. I looked at his chest.

"Go ahead," he said. "Touch it."

I raised my hand and touched his left pectoral. It was firm and smooth. I ran my fingers over his nipple.

"It's nice," I said.

"Feel my abs."

I ran my hand down his stomach. God it was fantastic. It was like a washboard. I rubbed my fingers over it and down below it. His stomach ended in a pronounced V.

"Amazing," I whispered.

"All it takes is a few million sit-ups."

I laughed.

"Well I'll have to get started."

He smiled at me and I knew something had changed between us.

"How 'bout let's try fishing?"

I wrapped my hook around my head, three trees and Austin's chest but after a while I got so I could cast out and hit the water. We sat in the sun and talked and laughed and had the most perfect day I'd ever had. We caught some fish and put them back.

At noon we ate some sandwiches and cookies. Then we lay on the grass and rested.

As usual Austin had his camo hat on. I noticed the Quaker Boy logo.

"Does that mean you're a Quaker?"

He laughed.

"No, that's a turkey call company. They make calls to fool turkeys."

"So you're not religious?"

"Ah am. Ah believe in God. Ah'm not sure about some of the things the church says though."

"Like what?"

"Some say that homosexuals and lesbians go to hell. Ah don't believe that."

"You know some homosexuals?"

"A few."

Huh. I didn't know what to say to that.

"How 'bout we take a swim, Ronan?"

"You mean naked?"

"Ain't noboby but me gonna see ya'll."

"I've never went naked outside."

"No time like now to try it."

He stood up and dropped his shorts and boxer briefs. His cock swung back and forth. I looked up at it.

Gulp...

If you enjoyed this sample then look for <u>First Love</u>.

AMY REDEK

His SPECIAL LESSONS

Quentin College was a place that I had taken a fancy to when I was studying for my doctorate at University and was very pleased when I received a letter asking me to attend an interview. I was one of twenty there that day and I progressed into the next interview of ten and finally for a third visit of just three of us for a position in such a prestigious college.

I was the last to be interviewed and I went into the Dean's office to find two other people sitting there along with the Dean himself, who had been present at my two previous visits. He was sitting behind his large desk and flanked by a man on his right and a woman on his left. I knew of them through my studies and the newspapers but waited until I was formally introduced to them before speaking.

'Sit down, Dr. Smith,' Dean Ainsworth said, indicating the chair placed before the desk. 'I am pleased to see that you made it to the last three and through your work, I'm sure you know Mrs. Cynthia Carrington who is attached to the Department of Education in the present government.' I nodded in her direction and gave her a small smile. 'And Sir Reginald Hudson, who, though in opposition at the moment, is the Chairman of the College Board of Governors.' I nodded in his direction and gave him the same smile.

'To recap for their benefit, you were born on the 14th May 1974 in London, christened Colin Franklin Smith and are now twenty-six years of age with both parents now deceased. You won high honours at college and obtained your doctorate at Oxford in the field of Political History on a brilliant thesis showing the parallels between the English Civil War and the American war of Independence. You have also written a book using these lines, which I myself have read and have ordered copies for the college library.

Now having seen you twice previously, I'll let my esteemed colleagues put forward their questions as to why you think you are fit for the position in this college. Mrs. Carrington, if you would be so kind as to lead off.'

He sat back with a smile on his face and listened to the questions that were fired at me for over half an hour and to my answers. They were very demanding and I gave the best answers that I could and felt mentally drained when it was over and shook hands all round before I left, being told that I would be notified within a week if I'd succeeded to the post or not.

I went back to London to my home in Chelsea. A house in Cheyne Walk left to me by my parents two years ago. My father had been a cardiac consultant, but his profession did nothing for him for he died of a heart attack at the age of sixty-one. Mother, with his loss, just seemed to pine away and so followed him two years later, but it was recorded as natural causes in her case.

That was two and a half years ago and so I went off to America to further my education in my field and had only been back in England for three months before applying for this doctorate post of Political History at Quentin College. In the States, I had attended Yale University, and by having the other side of the story as it were about what led up to the War of Independence, prompted me to write my thesis.

True to their word, I received a letter a week after my last interview from Dean Ainsworth congratulating me on securing the post and could take up residence whenever I wished for the incumbent had already retired. It was two weeks into the summer holidays and another four weeks before the new term year began; and as I didn't have any ties, immediately packed all that I would need and set off for the college.

Before the taxi driver could even begin to grumble about helping me get my two trunks down to his cab, I gave him a fiver and then had him drive me to the station where I had to get a porter to get them to my platform. The train I wanted was there and people were already boarding and I just had enough time to get my ticket and see the trunks put into the guards van.

If you enjoyed this sample then look for **His Special Lessons**.

4FUN PUBLISHING
ULTIMATE SUPER MEGA BUNDLE (30M/M BOOK BOX SET)

30 SHADES *of* GAY

BEST GAY STORIES OF 2015

Best Gay Stories of 2015 by three bestselling authors - Chris Johns, Gideon Elliot and Hank Brooks!

Things aren't always black and white. In gay love, there are various shades – sweet romance, erotic romance, there's domination and submission, interracial and inter-generational love stories, mystery, and just pure gay sex.

30 Shades of Gay is full of erotic male on male action that is so intense they fall on moral "gray areas".

30 M/M Super Mega Bundle gives you:
Border Patrol by Chris Johns
My Street Urchin by Chris Johns
Foreign Seduction by Chris Johns
Heart's Desire by Gideon Elliot
Unstable Emotion by Gideon Elliot
Erotic Aggression by Gideon Elliot
A Second Chance by Gideon Elliot
Sensual Surrender by Gideon Elliot
Forgiven by Hank Brooks
Divine Guilt by Hank Brooks
As You Are by Hank Brooks
Blood Work by Hank Brooks
Body Sweat by Hank Brooks
Harry's Trial by Hank Brooks
Fantasy Play by Hank Brooks
Secret Desire by Hank Brooks
Horny Visitors by Hank Brooks
Doubtful Heart by Hank Brooks
Pleasure Thirst by Hank Brooks
Fountain of Dreams by Hank Brooks
Year-Ender Surprise by Hank Brooks
Love Me If You Can by Hank Brooks
A Road To Nowhere by Hank Brooks

A Comfortable Sorrow by Hank Brooks
Elmwood Lane Secrets by Hank Brooks
Sensual Bet Rendezvous by Hank Brooks
A Commuter's Obsession by Hank Brooks
The Second Time Around by Hank Brooks
Another Chance of Delight by Hank Brooks
Backdoor Getaway Romance by Hank Brooks

If you enjoyed this sample then look for **30 Shades Of Gay.**

DONNY MUMFORD

OLIVER'S
ADVENTURES
A SEQUEL OF OLIVER'S WILDWOOD VACATION

This summer I worked, fell in and out of love, and had the time of my life vacationing at Wildwood New Jersey. Playtime is over now, though; tomorrow, I'm off to college. It's my freshman year at the University of Pennsylvania. All the preparations have been done and I'm nervously ready to go first thing in the morning. After a good night's sleep, we start out very early in the morning, like five o'clock, to be accurate. It's a five-hour drive for me in my Mini Cooper convertible. The car was a graduation present from my rich, albeit, mixed-up brother, Christian. I get to drive my car, and my parents insist on going with me, but in their SUV. Actually, me driving to college is a major deal and initially, I didn't think I'd be allowed. Freshmen living in dorms aren't normally permitted to have a car on campus. I side-stepped that technicality by applying for an "Assistance-Group" exception. I was accepted and got a sticker to park my car on campus. The Assistance Group is a very old campus organization with the mission of providing free assistance to incoming freshman. I'm now a member of this do-gooder group and it seems an easy way to get two credits each year, but mainly, I just wanted a parking pass for my car.

The Assistance Group members are asked to help another freshman in any number of ways. Maybe I'll be an aide to someone who needs help getting around, a student on crutches perhaps or a blind student, God forbid. Or maybe I'll have to chauffeur someone to a doctor's appointment or, hell, I don't know. If a student needs assistance, I'm their boy. I don't know that much about it because I didn't read all the materials they sent me. I also have no idea why I was admitted to the group, not that I really care. I've never been much of a joiner, but I really needed to have my car with me. How else would I get to see friends back home? So, no problem, dude, sign my ass up for whatever. The University of Pennsylvania is inside the city limits of Philadelphia so there aren't any rolling hills or expansive lawns on campus. There's a lot of cement and black-top and a lot of brick and ivy-covered old buildings. It's all new to me: the energy and excitement of big city life, plus the atmosphere of a major Ivy League university all wrapped together, wow! I liked everything about it when exploring the campus during my high school's senior class trip last May.

After arriving on campus, I need to wait forty-five minutes for my dad and mom to arrive. Dad drives agonizingly slow. Pretending I recently arrived myself, I tell dad, "I haven't had time to scope out the reception and admissions area, but I believe it's down this street." Mom smiles proudly, but my Dad makes a face like he know I'm full of it, and of course I am. I had plenty of time to drive around and find out where we should go. Registering turns out to be an extremely tedious experience, that's the best thing I can say about it. We won't be starting classes for two days, but there are orientation meetings that freshman should attend. That still leaves a lot of free time for me to get reacquainted with the campus. As part of registration, I'm assigned my dormitory building and my room, so off we go to have a look at my room and unpack the cars. When we get there, I'm pleased with both the dorm I'm in and the room. I immediately think about Cristobal, who I met during my class trip and with whom I had my very first sexual experience with. A very pleasant and exciting one it was too. I was in his dorm and right off it's apparent how much better my dormitory is than his. Better because my dormitory is centrally located near all the main classroom areas, dining rooms, recreation facilities, etc. But, by far, the number one reason my dorm is better is because there's a private bathroom for each of the rooms on the first floor. And, my room's on the first floor. No waiting for elevators, but much more importantly, no community bathing and shitting and such. On the wall next to the front door, a three-by-five card has been taped. On it, written in big block letters, "NICKERSON/GALLO".

If you enjoyed this sample then look for <u>Oliver's Adventures</u>.

WANT FREE COPIES OF MY BOOKS?

Just visit my blog and download free copies of my books:

http://gideon-elliot.awesomeauthors.org/gideon-elliot/

www.ingramcontent.com/pod-product-compliance
Lightning Source LLC
Chambersburg PA
CBHW071331130626
46556CB00004B/1855